Clifford AND THE GROUCHY NEIGHBORS

Story and pictures by Norman Bridwell

SCHOLASTIC INC.
New York Toronto London Auckland Sydney

Do you like dogs? I'm Emily Elizabeth, and
my dog is named Clifford. Most people like him.

ISBN 0-590-44261-9

70 69 68 67 66   16 17 18 19/0

But once we had neighbors

who didn't like Clifford at all.

Clifford wanted to make
friends with them anyhow.

Every day he went across the street to visit.
The neighbors acted as if he wasn't there.

Clifford isn't perfect.

He scratches himself as all dogs do.

Sometimes his fur would blow

into the neighbor's yard.

They didn't like that.

And sometimes Clifford snores at night.

Even a little snoring bothered them.

But Clifford liked them.
He liked to listen
to the woman singing.

Once he sang along.

Clifford couldn't seem
to do anything right.

When he sat by the fence,
the man complained that Clifford
blocked the sun from his plants.

One day Clifford noticed
that the tree blocked
the sun too. He took care
of the tree for the man.

But the people were not pleased.
Clifford had to put the tree back.

After that I told Clifford to stay away
from the neighbors. We saw them at the shopping
mall. We didn't go near them.

Then Clifford saw their shopping cart roll away while they opened their car. He tried to stop the cart.

What a mess.
Poor Clifford.
Poor people.

I told Clifford to never, never go near the neighbors again.

Clifford stayed on his side
of the street. He would sit
and watch the man feed the birds.
Clifford wished the man
liked him as much as he liked
the birds.

One day Clifford saw some workmen at the
neighbor's house. They were putting in new
water pipes. Clifford went
over to watch.

Clifford could see into the neighbor's yard.
Oh, oh — the birds were in trouble!

Clifford knew he couldn't go in the
neighbor's yard. So he picked up a water pipe
. . . took a deep breath . . .

and vacuumed the cat right out of the yard.
That was a very surprised cat.

The neighbors thanked Clifford
for saving the birds.

"He's not such a bad dog after all," they said.

Good old Clifford.

TYINYa